Gifts to Make

Written by Barbara Swett Burt

STECK-VAUGHN
ELEMENTARY · SECONDARY · ADULT · LIBRARY

A Harcourt Classroom Education Company

www.steck-vaughn.com

 Thumbprint Postcards

 A Leaf Mobile

 A Paperweight

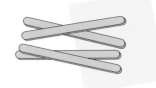 A Picture Frame

 A Picture Puzzle

 A Music Maker

Gifts to Give

Gifts are fun to give. They are also fun to make. Think of someone who is special to you. Maybe you can make a gift for that person.

How will you decide what to make? Think about what your special someone likes to do. Does that person like art? Does he or she like the outdoors? Think about these things when you choose a gift to make.

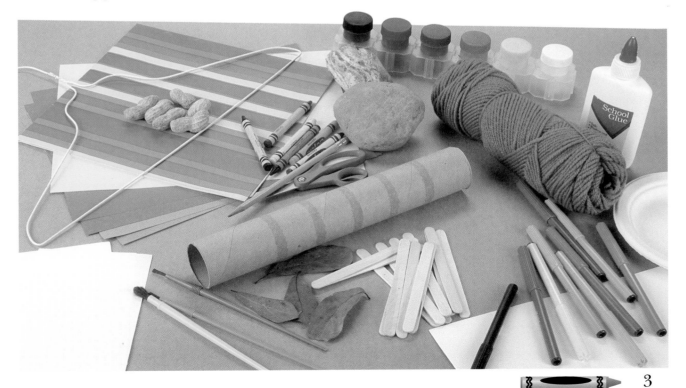

Thumbprint Postcards

Many people like to write and mail postcards. This is a kind of postcard that is fun to make. You will use your thumbprint to show that the card is from you.

Materials

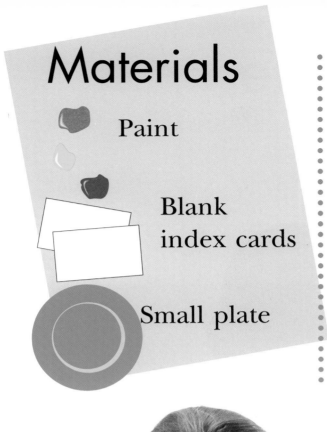

Paint

Blank
index cards

Small plate

1 Put a little paint on the plate.

2 Take out one blank index card.

3 Gently dip your thumb into the paint. Your thumb needs to be wet, but not dripping.

4 Press your thumb on the card. Let the paint dry.

5 Make more thumbprint cards the same way.

A Leaf Mobile

This is a gift for someone who likes the outdoors. It will make them feel like part of nature was brought inside.

Materials

4 or 5 Leaves

Colored paper

Pencil

Scissors

 Glue

Yarn   Hanger

1 Find four or five fallen leaves from outside.

2 Place each leaf on the colored paper and use the pencil to trace each.

3 Cut out each leaf outline.

4 Cut four or five pieces of yarn.

5 Glue a paper leaf to the end of each piece of yarn.

6 Tie each piece of yarn to the hanger.

A Paperweight

People who work inside may like thinking of the outdoors while they work. These people often have many papers on their desks. A paperweight made from a rock is a good gift for them.

Materials

Medium-sized rock

Paints

Paintbrush

1 Find a medium-sized rock.

2 Wash and dry the rock.

3 Use colorful paints to make pictures on the rock.

A Picture Frame

People like to have photos of special people and places. This frame is a gift to help someone think of you. It will make that person smile if you put your photo inside.

Materials

4 Craft sticks

Glue

Markers

Photo of yourself

1 Glue four craft sticks into the shape of a square.

2 Use different colored markers to draw pictures on the sticks.

3 Find a photo of yourself to glue inside.

A Picture Puzzle

Many people like to have fun working with puzzles. This gift is a game that has pieces to be put together. People can play with it again and again.

Materials

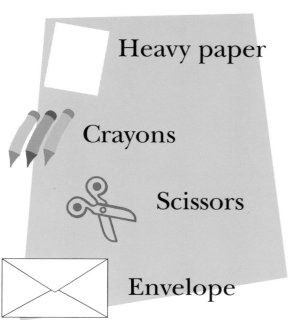

Heavy paper

Crayons

Scissors

Envelope

1 Use heavy paper to draw a picture on.

2 Color the picture.

3 Cut the picture into six pieces.

4 Place the picture pieces into an envelope.

A Music Maker

This gift is for the person who likes to make music. Most people like to listen to music. Some people can even make their own music.

Materials

Paper towel tube

Yarn

Wrapping paper

Peanuts
in the shell

1 Get a paper towel tube and a large sheet of wrapping paper.

2 Set the tube upright on the wrapping paper.

3 Place the peanuts inside the tube.

4 Pull the wrapping paper up and around the tube.

5 Squeeze the wrapping paper together at the top.

6 Tie the yarn around the top.

Gift Choices

Did one of the gifts in this book make you think of someone special? Which one would you like to make?

Before you give your gift to that person, wrap it up. Remember that giving a gift can be just as much fun as getting one.